THE PHYSICAL EDUCATION TEACHER

A Good Sport!

THE PHYSICAL EDUCATION TEACHER

A Good Sport!

by Patricia Lakin
pictures by Doug Cushman

RSVP

RAINTREE
STECK-VAUGHN
P U B L I S H E R S
The Steck-Vaughn Company

Austin, Texas

For Sue Sortino, a physical education teacher who encourages her students to train well and to respect all the participants on the field.

A Lucas • Evans Book

© Copyright 1995, Steck-Vaughn Company

Published by Raintree Steck-Vaughn Publishers, an imprint of Steck-Vaughn Company

Library of Congress Cataloging-in-Publication Data
Lakin, Pat.
A good sport / artist, Doug Cushman; author, Patricia Lakin.
p.   cm.— (My school)
Summary: While playing soccer with his classmates, Jeff demonstrates poor sportsmanship but gets some pointers on good behavior from his physical education teacher.
ISBN 0-8114-3870-8
[1. Soccer—Fiction.   2. Sportsmanship—Fiction.]   I. Cushman, Doug, ill.   II. Title.
III. Series: Lakin, Pat.   My school.
PZ7.L1586Go   1995
[E]—dc20   93-49845
CIP
AC

Printed and bound in the United States
1 2 3 4 5 6 7 8 9 0   99 98 97 96 95 94

Edward Lewis grabbed his whistle from the desk. The picture of him as a young Olympic runner stared down at him from the big poster on the wall. His students at Parkside Elementary School made him keep the poster up.

5

It was ten years ago when that gold medal had been placed around his neck. The American flag had waved high above his head. It was a moment he would never forget.

Now, being a physical education teacher was what he liked best. He went outside and set up a goal box at each end of the field.

"Hi, kids!" Edward greeted the third graders coming onto the field. "Wow! You look tired already."

"We just had a game of tag at recess," said Harriet.

"And I won," said Caroline, wheeling herself beside them.

"Good for you, Caroline," said Edward. "Are the hand exercises I taught you helping?"

"I'll say," said Tim. "We call Caroline the 'speedster.'"

Edward blew his whistle. "Please sit in a circle on the ground. Caroline, you can be next to me."

"What are we doing today?" asked Lucy.

"We're going to play soccer," said Edward. "Who has seen or played the game?"

A hand shot up.

"Me," said Jeff. "I play with my older brother. He's in a league. I'm great at this game."

"Glad to hear it," said Edward.

"I should probably be goalkeeper," added Jeff.

"Mr. Lewis, is soccer the game where you can't touch the ball with your hands?" asked Rachel.

"Right," said Edward.

"Good," said Lucy. "I stink at catching."

"You use your feet," said Edward. He showed everyone how to pass, kick, or stop the ball by using a different part of the foot to do each job.

"Now here are the basic rules," said Edward. "There are two teams. You want to get the soccer ball into the other team's goal. That's how you score."

"But goalkeepers try to stop the ball from going in," said Jeff. "I've gotta have that position."

"Okay, Jeff," said Edward.

"Can we steal the ball from the person who has it?" asked Rachel.

"Sure can. That's the whole idea. But remember, you can't touch the ball with your hands."

"Goalkeepers can," said Jeff.

"He's right," said Edward. "Now, who remembers our most important rule?"

"Respect all the players," said Tim.

"Exactly," said Edward. "Caroline, want to be referee?"

"Sure, Mr. Lewis."

While the kids did warm-up exercises, Edward told Caroline how to referee.

The class chose Rachel and Tim as team captains.

Edward placed the ball in the center of the playing field.
He whistled for the game to start. Rachel got to the ball first.

13

Harriet kicked it away from her.

"Pass it to me!" Tim shouted to Harriet.

Harriet whacked it, and the ball headed for Tim. He lined it up and aimed straight for the goal box. But Jeff ran forward, pushing Tim. Tim lost his balance and fell.

Edward's whistle cut through the noise.

14

"Freeze!" he called. Everyone stood like statues. "Jeff, you're out of the game."

"What?" Jeff got red in the face. "I just saved my team!"

"Winning isn't the only goal, Jeff."

"Okay! Okay!" he mumbled. "I won't do it again."

Tim rubbed his leg. "Let him play," he said. "I'm not hurt."

"One more chance, then," said Edward. "But I'd like Rachel to be goalkeeper. Switch places," said Edward.

Jeff scuffed his feet as he walked across the field.

Lucy kicked the ball first. "To me! To me!" yelled Jeff.

16

Lucy looked confused.

"Come on! Don't play that way!" yelled Jeff.

Lucy kicked the ball. It flew into the air. Jeff caught it in his hands.

"Foul!" yelled Caroline.

"It was NOT FOUL!" screamed Jeff. "She wasn't supposed to kick it. I had no choice." He held the ball very tight.

"No catching with your hands," said Lucy.

"Goalkeepers can!" yelled Jeff.

"You're not the goalkeeper now," said Caroline.

Jeff threw the ball across the field. "Who wants to play your dumb game anyway? I'm sitting out."

Jeff stomped over to the sidelines and sat in a heap.

Edward started the game again. Everyone, except Jeff, had
a great time and got a good workout.

20

"So long," said Edward when their class was over.

Jeff just slunk off the field. This wasn't the first time Jeff had behaved badly. It had also happened a few months ago, during a softball game. Edward thought it might be a good idea to ask the school psychologist for advice. She was going to be at Parkside the next day.

But for now he had to get the gym ready for the second grade. Edward pulled out the mats, the balance beams, and the horses for their gymnastics class.

At four-thirty, Edward got ready to go home. He did warm-up exercises before his daily three-mile run.

He walked down the hall, stopping when he heard the voices of Jeff and Tim. Edward peeked around the corner. They were painting pictures for the art bulletin board.

"I'll show you again how to draw a soccer ball," said Tim. "We'll try it from a different angle."

"Forget it. You gave me a bad brush," Jeff yelled. "I can't draw a soccer ball, and I can't kick a soccer ball. I can't do anything right."

"It's not my fault if you want to be perfect at everything," said Tim.

"He's sure right about that," said Edward. "Sorry to interrupt, boys. What's the trouble?"

"Mr. Lewis," Jeff looked up at him, "you're a champion Olympic runner. I'll bet you were always terrific."

"Hey! I wasn't so great when I was your age. I thought I knew everything," said Edward. "When things went wrong, I used to blame my teammates."

"Like you did in soccer today," said Tim, looking at Jeff.

Jeff was quiet for a moment. "What happened to make you change?" Jeff asked Edward.

"Well, just because I was thinking only of myself, I lost a big race. I also lost my best friend because I was showing off," said Edward. "After a while I began to understand that I had to concentrate on being a better runner—for my team—and not just on being a star."

"You didn't care about winning?" asked Jeff.

"Of course! But I finally began to appreciate that great feeling of pulling together with my teammates to win."

Jeff was quiet again. "I guess I was only thinking about myself today," he said finally.

"Jeff, if you respect the abilities of your teammates, and not just your own, you will always be a good sport."

"And maybe a pro soccer player?" asked Jeff.

"And maybe a pro soccer player," echoed Edward, smiling.

Duties of a Physical Education Teacher

- Teach movement, skills, games, and their rules

- Prepare daily lesson plans

- Report any repairs that the gym or equipment needs

- Set up specific gym equipment for each class

- Enforce safety rules for each activity

- Report on each student's abilities

- Supervise team tryouts

- Coach various teams

- Attend faculty meetings

- Submit list to the principal for any materials needed